Dear Parent:
Your child's love of reading starts here!

Every child learns to read in a different way and at his or her own speed. Some go back and forth between reading levels and read favorite books again and again. Others read through each level in order. You can help your young reader improve and become more confident by encouraging his or her own interests and abilities. From books your child reads with you to the first books he or she reads alone, there are I Can Read Books for every stage of reading:

SHARED READING
Basic language, word repetition, and whimsical illustrations, ideal for sharing with your emergent reader

BEGINNING READING
Short sentences, familiar words, and simple concepts for children eager to read on their own

READING WITH HELP
Engaging stories, longer sentences, and language play for developing readers

READING ALONE
Complex plots, challenging vocabulary, and high-interest topics for the independent reader

ADVANCED READING
Short paragraphs, chapters, and exciting themes for the perfect bridge to chapter books

I Can Read Books have introduced children to the joy of reading since 1957. Featuring award-winning authors and illustrators and a fabulous cast of beloved characters, I Can Read Books set the standard for beginning readers.

A lifetime of discovery begins with the magical words **"I Can Read!"**

Visit www.icanread.com for information on enriching your child's reading experience.

The BEST CHEF in Second Grade

story by Katharine Kenah

pictures by Abby Carter

HarperCollins*Publishers*

For Maura, Eva, Katie, and Ben . . .
my backyard buddies, with love
—K.K.

For Lauren, Leah, Jamie, and Carter
—A.C.

 Printed in the United States of America. For information address HarperCollins Children's Books, a division of HarperCollins Publishers, 1350 Avenue of the Americas, New York, NY 10019. www.harpercollinschildrens.com

Library of Congress Cataloging-in-Publication Data is available.
ISBN-10: 0-06-053561-X (trade bdg.) — ISBN-13: 978-0-06-053561-2 (trade bdg.)
ISBN-10: 0-06-053562-8 (lib. bdg.) — ISBN-13: 978-0-06-053562-9 (lib. bdg.)

1 2 3 4 5 6 7 8 9 10 ❖ First Edition

Contents

Chef Antonia 7

Too Rosy 16

Cupcakes and Meatballs 24

Someone Else's Sister 38

Chef Antonia

Ollie wanted to be the best
at something in second grade.
He was not the best reader.
He was not the best runner.
He was not the best artist.
Everyone else in Room 75
seemed to shine.

One Tuesday Mr. Hopper said,
"I have a surprise for you.
We will have a guest on Friday.
Chef Antonia is coming!"

“Chef Antonia?” asked Miguel.

“From the TV show?” asked Sam.

“The real one?” asked Luna.

“The one and only,” said Mr. Hopper.

“She is going to cook

something special for us.”

Ollie could not believe his ears.

He loved Chef Antonia!

She threw food in the air.

She set desserts on fire.

Ollie watched her show every day.

"But she is famous," Nina said.
"Why is she coming to our class?"
Mr. Hopper just grinned and said,
"Let's surprise Chef Antonia
and cook something special for her."

“I don’t know how to cook,”

moaned Sophie.

“It will be fun,” said Mr. Hopper.

“Find something that everyone

in your family likes to eat.

We will share our Family Favorites

with Chef Antonia on Friday.”

Ollie loved to mix and stir.

He loved to sprinkle and mash.

The treats he made for his family
were tasty and beautiful.
Ollie loved to cook
more than anything in the world.
But what was his Family Favorite?
He had only three days to find out!

Too Rosy

"What is our Family Favorite?"

Ollie asked at supper that night.

"Favorite what?" asked his father.

"Food," said Ollie.

"I need to find a dish we all like."

Ollie's mother licked her lips.

"I love Aunt Ida's Bean Surprise,"

she said.

"I hate beans," said Rosy.

While they were doing the dishes,
Ollie's father said,
"I love my cousin Charley's
Five-Alarm Chili."
"It's too red," said Rosy.

At bedtime Ollie asked,
"What about Grandma's
Double Delight Chocolate Cake?"
"It is yummy," said his mother.
"It is tasty," said his father.
"I like vanilla," said Rosy.

The next morning
Rosy held her bowl of oatmeal
in front of Ollie.
"It needs a face," she said.

Ollie reached for the berries.
One by one he put them
on Rosy's oatmeal.
Soon a blueberry face
was smiling at his sister.
"Thanks!" said Rosy.

Ollie looked around the table.

"Do you *all* like oatmeal?" he asked.

"Sure," said his mother.

"Sure," said his father.

"No," said Rosy.

"I only like the face."

She picked off the berries

and ate them one by one.

"We are a family," shouted Ollie,
"but we have no favorite!"
He dumped his oatmeal in the sink
and stomped outside to the bus.

Cupcakes and Meatballs

On Thursday Ollie's class
pushed their desks into squares.
They made red-and-white tablecloths,
cardboard candles, and paper flowers.
"Great job!" said Mr. Hopper.
"It looks like a restaurant in here.
Now it is time to get to work."

They opened their science books.

"Who can tell us about clams?"

asked Mr. Hopper.

"They go into my grandpa's soup,"

Miguel said proudly.

"Clam chowder is my Family

Favorite!"

Ollie did not say anything.

Next they did math problems
using measuring cups and spoons.
"We bake with these at home,"
said Luna.
"Cupcakes sprinkled with stars
are my Family Favorite!"
Ollie did not say anything.

They tossed basketballs at recess.
"Guess what I am bringing
for Chef Antonia," said Nina.
"What?" everyone asked.
"Meatballs!" Nina smiled.
"I am bringing homemade bread,"
said Sam.

"I am bringing cherry pie,"
said Sophie.
"Does everyone in your family
like pie?" asked Ollie.
"Yes," said Sophie.
"Pie is my Family Favorite."

By noon Ollie felt too awful to eat.
He made aliens out of his lunch.
“Are you all right, Ollie?” asked Nina.
“I’m fine,” he said.

But Ollie was not fine.
Everyone in his class
had a Family Favorite.
Everyone *except* Ollie.

That night after supper,
Ollie went to find his mother.
She was reading a book.
“Mom?” asked Ollie.
“What is your favorite food?”
“I like macaroni,” she said.

Ollie went to find his father.

He was taking a bath.

“Dad!” Ollie yelled.

“What is your favorite food?”

Ollie’s father answered, “Cheese!”

Ollie marched into Rosy's room.

She was painting her dollhouse.

"Rosy?" asked Ollie.

"What is your favorite food?"

"Macaroni and cheese," said Rosy.

"But only if it has a face."

Ollie dashed to the kitchen.

He mixed and stirred.

He sprinkled and mashed.

Soon a pan of macaroni and cheese was cooling on the counter.

“It looks so golden,” said his mother.

“It looks so creamy,” said his father.

“It was my idea,” said Rosy.

Someone Else's Sister

On Friday morning,
Family Favorites filled Room 75.
They looked and smelled wonderful.
Suddenly Ollie worried
that his macaroni and cheese
was too silly for Chef Antonia.
He put the pan down
without taking off its cover.

There was a noise in the hallway.

A huge cart rumbled through the door.

Bowls wobbled and spoons rattled.

Chef Antonia was in Room 75!

Chef Antonia looked
at each Family Favorite.
“Lovely, lovely!” she said.
Ollie did not say anything.
He stood back and watched.

When Chef Antonia picked up his pan,
she pulled off the cover and gasped.
"Look at this!" she exclaimed.
"It is macaroni and cheese . . .
with a *face*!"
Everyone started to laugh.

“Whose Family Favorite is this?”

asked Chef Antonia.

“Mine,” Ollie said quietly.

His cheeks turned red.

He wanted to hide.

Chef Antonia held up Ollie's pan.

"Look at those colors," she said.

"Look at that smile.

This dish was made by a *chef*!"

Everyone clapped and cheered.

"When Chef Antonia was little,
she liked faces on her food too,"
said Mr. Hopper.
Ollie's eyes opened wide.
"How do you know?" he asked.

Mr. Hopper smiled.
“I know because Chef Antonia
is my little sister,” he said.
“Now let’s cook something special.”

Ollie put on an apron
and stood beside Chef Antonia.
It did not matter what they made.
He was ready to help.
Ollie loved to cook
more than anything else in the world.
He was the best chef in second grade.